THE G...

"I like CHOOSE ... books because the... ...rises. I can't wait to read more.

—Cary Romanos, age 12

"Sometimes you get attacked by sharks and squid. I went down to Atlantis five times."

—Sebastian Stanley, age 10

"A very adventurous book, makes you think thoroughly before making a decision."

—Hassan Stevenson, age 11

"I read five different stories in one night and that's a record for me. The different endings were fun."

—Timmy Sullivan, age 9

"It was great fun! I liked the idea of making my own decisions."

—Anthony Ziccardi, age 11

AND TEACHERS LIKE THIS SERIES TOO:

"We have read and reread, worn thin, loved, loaned, bought for others, and donated to school libraries our CHOOSE YOUR OWN ADVENTURE books."

CHOOSE YOUR OWN ADVENTURE— AND MAKE READING MORE FUN!

Bantam Books in the Choose Your Own Adventure Series
Ask your bookseller for the books you have missed

THE MYSTERY OF CHIMNEY ROCK

EDWARD PACKARD

ILLUSTRATED BY PAUL GRANGER

BANTAM BOOKS
TORONTO • NEW YORK • LONDON

RL5, IL 4+

THE MYSTERY OF CHIMNEY ROCK
A Bantam Book / January 1980
2nd printing . . . . . February 1980
3rd printing . . . . April 1980
4th printing . . . . July 1980
5th printing . . . September 1980
6th printing . . . . December 1980

"The Adventures of You Series" is a Montgomery
Associates, Inc. Trademark for reader participation
fiction. Original conception of Edward Packard.

Artist: Paul Granger

ISBN 0-553-14001-9

Published simultaneously in the United States and Canada

PRINTED IN THE UNITED STATES OF AMERICA

15 14 13 12 11 10 9 8

THE MYSTERY
OF CHIMNEY ROCK

WARNING!!!!

Do not read this book straight through from beginning to end! These pages contain many different adventures you can go on in Chimney Rock. From time to time as you read along, you will be asked to make a choice. Your choice may lead to success or disaster!

The adventures you take are a result of your choice. *You* are responsible because *you* choose! After you make your choice, follow the instructions to see what happens to you next.

Remember—you cannot go back! Think carefully before you make a move! One mistake can be your last . . . or it *may* lead you to fame and fortune!

2

Vacation is here and you're visiting your cousins Michael and Jane for a few days at their new home in Connecticut. Soon after you arrive, they take you on a tour of their neighborhood, along shady streets lined with cozy houses with neatly-trimmed lawns. At the top of a hill you notice a huge stone house unlike any you have ever seen. It has turrets, walled terraces and a square tower that looks like a giant chimney. Some of the windows are boarded up and others are hidden by vines and bushes. There is a big dog chained in front of the little cottage nearby, and you ask your cousins if anyone lives in the main house.

"Chimney Rock? Most people around here wouldn't live there for a million dollars," Michael says.

"It's supposed to be cursed," Jane adds. "They say that some people who have gone inside have never been seen again. What happened to them is still a mystery."

Go on to the next page.

"You see," Michael exclaims, "Mrs. Bigley lived in Chimney Rock alone with her cat for many years. When she died, she left instructions in her will that the cat could live there for the rest of its life. People say that she put a curse on the house so that no one would bother the cat."

"Haven't the police investigated?" you ask.

"The police never found anyone—only the cat," Michael says, "but some people say Mrs. Bigley never died at all—and that she's still living there herself!"

"What does the caretaker say?" you ask.

"He doesn't say anything," Michael replies. "Some say he's crazy, and some say he's just mean, but I guess he's afraid of the curse too, because I hear he won't set foot inside Chimney Rock."

"You're not kidding?" you ask.

"If you think we're kidding," Michael says, "why don't *you* go inside?"

If you say, "I'll do it," turn to page 4.

If you say, "no thanks," turn to page 6.

"I'll do it," you say.

"OK," Michael replies. "When are you going?
Jane and I will watch you."

"We'll want to say good-by to you," Jane says.

You take time to get a flashlight from the house,
and then the three of you set off for Chimney
Rock. You feel a bit nervous, but it's a beautiful
day, and you keep telling yourself there is really
nothing to worry about.

As you approach it, the house looks bleak and
forbidding, like some medieval fortress. A dark
cloud passes in front of the sun. The wind blows
dust in your eyes. You wish you hadn't agreed to
go inside. But it's too late to back out now, so,
while Michael and Jane watch from a distance, you
walk around the house and try all the doors. Every
one of them is locked except for one in the back of

the house. You wave to your cousins, open the door and walk into an entryway that leads to a large kitchen. There are rows of sinks and counters and a huge black oven. The floor is laid with dark red tiles, many of them chipped or loose. The windows are covered with cloth shades, and you raise one of them to let in more light.

On your right is a flight of steps leading from the kitchen upstairs; to the left is a swinging door, which you imagine leads to the dining room.

If you go up the stairs, turn to page 8.

If you go through the swinging door into the dining room, turn to page 10.

When you say "no thanks," Michael replies, "Well, I don't blame you."

"I'll go in," Jane says, "even if you two are afraid, but only on one condition! That you'll come after me if I don't come out within five minutes."

You and Michael can hardly refuse, so the three of you walk up the road to Chimney Rock. There is no sign of the caretaker or anyone else. You circle the house, trying all the doors. Jane finds one that is unlocked. While you and Michael watch, she opens it and walks inside.

You suspect that Jane is standing just inside the door and will come out when the five minutes are up. But five, then six and then seven minutes go by. You exchange worried glances with Michael.

"I guess we better go in after her," you say.

"I'm going to get help," he replies. "You stand watch."

Before you can answer, he goes running off toward the road.

If you go inside after Jane right away, turn to page 12.

If you wait for Michael to get help, turn to page 11.

8

You start up the stairs, trying to make as little noise as possible. The railing is falling off, and the dust and cobwebs get thicker each step of the way until you reach the landing, which is dimly lit by pale yellow light coming through a circular stained glass window. Steps continue up in two directions from the landing, but on the same level is a hall leading to a door that is slightly ajar. You walk up to it and gently push it open.

Before you is a dingy room filled with furniture and trunks, an old-fashioned radio, a grandfather clock, a rocking horse, some coils of rope, piles of books and, on the dusty floor, a dead mouse. In the back of the room is a large closet.

If you open the closet door, turn to page 14.

If you go back to the landing, turn to page 15.

You walk through the swinging door and into an elegant dining room. A splendid crystal chandelier hangs over the long oak table. Double bay windows are partly hidden by dark green, satin curtains. A bottle of wine rests on a silver tray on the sideboard. Next to it is a bright green china cat.

You sit down at the table and ponder the situation. There is a small, brass bell within reach, and on impulse, you ring it.

Within a few moments, a door you hadn't noticed before opens, and a thin, young woman walks in. She is wearing a black dress and a little white hat in the fashion of a maid.

"Oh," she says, looking at you with surprise, "I didn't know Mrs. Bigley was expecting a guest today. I'm Lena. May I bring you anything? Perhaps cheese and crackers—you must be hungry."

*If you accept her offer,
turn to page 16.*

*If you decide to question her first,
turn to page 17.*

While you are waiting for Michael, you walk around the house, tapping on the windows and doors. They are locked—even the back door through which Jane entered. She must be imprisoned inside.

You see Jervis, the caretaker, going into his cottage. Maybe he will help you.

But there is another possibility. There is a thick vine wrapped around a pillar that supports a balcony over the side porch. It looks as though you could climb it and perhaps get into the house through the windows off the balcony.

If you go to the caretaker's cottage and ask Jervis for help, turn to page 22.

If you climb up the vine to the balcony, turn to page 21.

12

Almost as soon as you step inside the house, you hear a muffled cry for help. It's Jane! Following the sound of her voice, you run through the kitchen, fling open the swinging door to the dining room, and make your way through the dark, musty library and into the front hall. You find her there, huddled behind the grand staircase.

"What happened? Are you all right?" you ask.

"If only you can help me!" she cries. "I'm trapped."

"Trapped?"

"Yes! I was looking around the house and I found a cat sitting right where we are now—it must be Melissa—and I went up to pat her, but she gave me a terrible look; she seemed to be laughing at me. Then she began pacing back and forth—as if there were bars there between us. Finally, she went away, but *I feel as if the bars are still there,* and that if I try to go through them something terrible will happen."

You are unable to convince Jane that she has nothing to fear.

If you try to force Jane across the bars to prove they are not real, turn to page 19.

If you say you will go get help, turn to page 20.

You make your way through the furniture scattered about the room and open the door to the closet. It smells of moth balls and is filled with clothes, some very old, some quite new. You notice a policeman's uniform, and a large key ring with three keys on it hanging from a nail.

You are suddenly startled by a squeaky noise. It is only a mouse scurrying across the room. You walk back toward the door. The mouse comes running right at you! You step back, ready to kick it away, but suddenly it rolls over on its side, dead.

You rush out of the room toward the stairs. Then, as you collect your wits, you remember the keys, and wonder if they might come in handy.

*If you go back for the keys,
turn to page 24.*

*If you continue down the stairs to
the kitchen, turn to page 25.*

The storeroom is a creepy place; you are glad to be out of it. When you reach the landing, you notice something you hadn't seen before—a brass ring set in the floor. You tug at the ring, and a square portion of the floor comes up. You pull it wide open, exposing a narrow circular staircase leading to a room below.

There is just enough light to see by, and you start climbing down the stairs, curious as to where they lead. Suddenly, you hear a crash overhead. The trap door has slammed shut.

If you go back and make sure you can open the trap door, turn to page 26.

If you continue down the stairs, turn to page 28.

You really are hungry and thank Lena for the offer, but ask if she has anything else besides cheese and crackers. Smiling, she goes out and returns a moment later with some delicious-looking brownies. You pick one up and take a very small bite. It tastes even better than it looks, and you can't resist eating it all.

In a moment your eyes become blurry. You feel as if you have been drugged. You ring the bell, but Lena does not return. You get up and start toward the door, but you feel yourself falling.

Sometime later you awaken, feeling weak and confused. It is pitch dark.

If you try to sleep until morning, turn to page 27.

If you try to grope your way out, turn to page 31.

"No thanks," you reply. "I had heard this house is occupied only by Mrs. Bigley's cat. But I guess Mrs. Bigley still lives here too. If I'd known that, I wouldn't have barged in."

"Oh, Mrs. Bigley doesn't mind. I'm sure she was expecting you. She *loves* to have visitors," Lena says.

"I'm glad of that," you reply. "But where is she?"

"She is upstairs in the music room, playing the piano," Lena answers.

*If you decide to leave Chimney Rock,
turn to page 32.*

*If you decide to go to the music room,
turn to page 34.*

Before Jane realizes what you are doing, you pull her through the imaginary bars.

"Melissa must have put a spell on me," she says.

"Just a little spell," you reply. "Let's find that cat. We'll end its curse on Chimney Rock."

At that moment, you hear a meowing from the top of the stairs. The two of you run up to the top landing.

"You look to the right and I'll go left," Jane says.

There is no sign of the cat in the hall, so you look into a bedroom with its door open. Still no luck. You run to the other hall to see how Jane is doing, but she's nowhere in sight. You call out to her. You open every door that is not locked and look inside, but she does not answer. You walk back toward the stairs and jump with a start as a mouse runs past; then hurry on for a few steps . . .

Suddenly, standing before you, is a tall, elderly woman dressed in black, her hair swept back in a bun. Her burning green eyes seem to stare right through you.

So this is Mrs. Bigley! She never died after all. She looks like a witch! But of course witches don't really exist. Or do they?

If you speak to Mrs. Bigley,
turn to page 35.

If you run down the stairs,
turn to page 36.

You run back toward the kitchen door. As you go through the study, you see an old woman, dressed all in black. Her face is pale, and her reddish-white hair is swept back in a bun. So this is Mrs. Bigley! She looks so frightening, you would think she is a witch, if witches really existed.

"How nice it is to have visitors," she says in a raspy voice. "You've been in the house quite a while, haven't you? I hardly knew where to find you; you've been running around as quietly as a mouse. Well, now that you're here, come with me to the pantry. I have some cheese and crackers I know you will like!"

"Thanks, but I'm very anxious to help my cousin Jane," you say. "She's in the front hall. I'm afraid she is losing her mind. She thinks she is imprisoned by bars. But she really isn't."

"Oh, I can take care of her. Don't worry," Mrs. Bigley replies. "Just sit down and enjoy some cheese and crackers and I promise you I'll find Jane."

If you decide to humor Mrs. Bigley and have some cheese and crackers, turn to page 37.

If you try to get away, turn to page 38.

You summon up your strength. Clinging tightly as you climb, you manage to pull yourself up to the second story balcony. You climb over the railing and step on to a small porch.

Looking through a window, you observe a mouse scurrying around on the bare wood floor.

You find the window unlocked. It opens easily and you could climb right in. Yet your hands feel clammy; your heart is pounding. As you lift the window open, you sense an evil presence within the room.

If you climb in, turn to page 42.

If you call for Jane through the open window, turn to page 41.

You cross the meadow to the cottage and knock loudly on the door.

In a moment a heavyset man wearing a dirty plaid shirt opens the door. His face is pale and fat. His eyes are pink, like a pig's. Behind him is a huge dog—a mastiff—chained to a radiator. The dog growls menacingly, but does not move.

"What do you want?" Jervis asks gruffly.

"My cousin Jane is trapped in the house and I'm worried about her. Would you please unlock it and help me find her?"

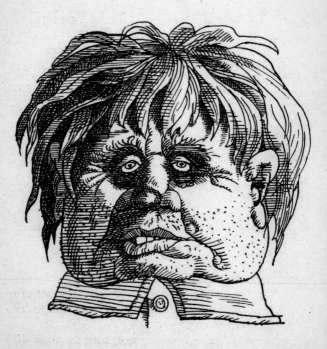

"She should not be in there. Even I don't set foot in that house," Jervis says.

"Why not?" you ask.

"The mistress would put me away."

"You mean you just take care of the grounds?"

"Aye, and bring them food and things."

"But who takes care of the house?"

"It's taken care of all right, and so is anybody who goes inside. That's why I'll let you in, if you want."

If you ask Jervis to let you inside the house, turn to page 39.

If not, turn to page 40.

Cautiously, you retrace your steps to the storeroom closet, take the key ring, and return to the landing. At the top of one of the two flights of stairs leading upward, you make out the silhouette of a large black cat, its green eyes shining in the gloom of the hall.

Its back arched, its teeth bared, the cat hisses softly as you approach.

If you call to the cat to show you are friendly, turn to page 44.

If you retreat down the stairs to the kitchen, turn to page 46.

You continue down the stairs. As you take your first step into the kitchen, you see a man peering through a window. He is a large, heavy man and his square jaw and squinty eyes give him a sinister appearance. He surveys the room and his gaze rests upon you. It is Jervis, the caretaker.

Although you stand motionless in the shadows, you are certain he has seen you. In a moment, he leaves the window. He must be coming around to the back door.

If you try to evade him by hiding somewhere in the house, turn to page 48.

If you decide it would be better to go to the door and meet him, turn to page 49.

You climb up the stairs and push against the trap door. It won't budge. You push again, with all your might. Suddenly, the door flies open. You quickly climb out and find yourself looking into the burning, green eyes of a black cat—Melissa! Startled by your appearance, she arches her back and hisses, then leaps at you, claws extended. You reel back and she scampers off.

You follow her quickly through the kitchen and into the dining room where you lose sight of her. Then you hear the voice of an old woman calling, in a cackling voice, "Melissa, where are you?"

If you call out—"Hello,"
turn to page 54.

If you try to find where
the voice was coming from,
turn to page 50.

You soon fall asleep again. When you awaken, the house is darker than the day before. It is raining outdoors. You are anxious to get out, and you run to the kitchen door. You pull it open, only to find the entry blocked by the huge figure of Jervis, the caretaker.

"You're a brave one, coming in here," he says.

"So I've learned. I think someone drugged me," you reply.

Jervis laughs menacingly. He holds his arm across the door, blocking you from getting past.

"Drugged, you say," he says. "You'd be lucky if that's all it were."

"What do you mean?" you ask.

"You've not been drugged. You are *possessed*—possessed by the cat devil. Your only chance is to stare down the cat till it gives in, or you will be cursed the rest of your life."

"Why should I believe such a story?" you ask.

"Can't you see," Jervis says, pressing in so close that you take a step backward, *"I'm* cursed." Then in a calmer tone he says—"The maid you saw— *she's* been cursed, too!"

Jervis talks so earnestly that you begin to think there could be something to what he says.

If you tell Jervis you will go find the cat and stare it down, turn to page 56.

If you decide to try to get past Jervis and escape, turn to page 57.

Figuring you can open the trap door easily enough later, you continue down into the basement of the house. The staircase is rickety; its wooden supports are rotted. Proceeding carefully, you reach the dirt floor of the basement. A little light comes in through several windows high above. The windows are slits, too narrow to climb through, even if you could reach them. Except for a few pieces of old furniture, a furnace, and overhead pipes and wires, the basement seems bare. Then from somewhere in the shadows, you hear the meowing of a cat.

*If you try to find the cat,
turn to page 52.*

*If you start up the stairway,
turn to page 55.*

You grope your way along in the dark, trying to find the swinging door to the kitchen. A hand clutches your arm. You feel like screaming.

"Help," a voice calls almost in a whisper.

"Who are you?" you reply.

"I'm Lena, Mrs. Bigley's maid. I was afraid to speak before. I cannot escape without your help."

"You can just walk out of the house," you say.

"I wish I could, but I can't. I'm under the curse . . ."

"But can't Mrs. Bigley help?"

"*Mrs. Bigley?* Don't you understand?"

Lena bursts into tears. You try to comfort her. Finally, she steadies herself and renews her grip on your sleeve.

"Please," she cries. "If you will only carry the cat out of the house, I will be saved. *Will you help me?*"

If you say "yes," turn to page 58.

If you try to reason with her, turn to page 59.

"Thanks again," you say, "but I think I better be going."

You get up and start toward the kitchen.

"Oh, I wouldn't go that way," Lena says. "Jervis, the caretaker, is there."

"Why should I be afraid of him?" you ask. "He has no right to keep me here."

"Sh. You must not make so much noise," Lena says. "Mrs. Bigley would be very angry if she knew you were trying to leave."

You say nothing more, but start toward the kitchen. For the first time, you notice a portrait on the wall of a tall slender woman, dressed in black and gray and holding a large black cat in her lap. As you walk toward the kitchen, you can't help keeping your eyes on the portrait, and the eyes in the portrait seem to follow you. The sensation it produces is so eerie and unpleasant you begin to feel ill.

Go on to the next page.

With your eyes fixed upon the portrait, you reel against the sideboard. You put your hand out to balance yourself and knock over the green china cat. You watch it fly through the air and crash into dozens of pieces. Lena stands looking at you, speechless, her face white with horror.

If you start picking up the pieces, turn to page 60.

If you decide to try to get out as fast as you can, turn to page 61.

"Then I shall pay my respects to her," you say.

You are curious to meet the mysterious Mrs. Bigley and dispel the myth about the curse. You get directions to the music room from Lena and find your way to the front hall and up the wide oak staircase to the second floor. From the upper hall you can hear the soft, plunking sounds of an old piano.

Turn to page 69.

"I'm sorry to intrude," you say, "but I must find my cousin Jane. She was here a moment ago and now she is missing."

"Oh, you needn't worry about your little friend," Mrs. Bigley says. "She must have run downstairs. We'll go and look for her."

Relieved at Mrs. Bigley's words, you start down the stairs, thinking she will follow. After a few steps you glance back. She is gone. Confused, you continue on to the first floor and into the library. It looks as if you will have to search the house on your own.

Turn to page 66.

You run down the stairs and enter the library, where you almost collide with a slim, young woman in a black dress with white lace and a little white hat.

"You gave me such a start," she says.

"I'm sorry about that," you reply, "but I'm trying to find my cousin Jane. Who are you?"

"My name is Lena. I am Mrs. Bigley's maid. Do you know that there is a policeman outside? I just saw him through the window. There is a boy with him. He'll be coming in the back door. I must let him in."

"Yes, he'll help me find Jane," you say.

"He will never be able to help you. You must stay out of sight. That is your only chance."

Lena seems to make no sense; yet somehow you feel she is speaking the truth.

If you decide to talk to the policeman, turn to page 66.

If you decide to go into another part of the house and look for Jane, turn to page 67.

You go into the pantry with Mrs. Bigley. Some crackers and cheese are already on the table. You decide to eat one cracker and no more. As soon as you take your first bite, you feel dizzy.

Your vision is blurred, but, as well as you can tell, everything around you looks as if it is growing in size. The fuzzy outline of Mrs. Bigley seems to tower above you. You wonder if you have been poisoned, but you can't think straight.

You jump down from your chair and run as fast as you can out of the dining room and into the study. You hear sounds behind you. Mrs. Bigley must be chasing you. You dare not look back. For an instant, you realize you should not be afraid of an old woman, but you *are* afraid.

Ahead of you is a small passageway you didn't notice before. It looks almost like a tunnel—an escape route. You scamper inside. You have to crawl, but gradually it seems to get larger, much larger, so that you can almost stand up. Suddenly you realize that your surroundings have not been getting larger; you have been getting smaller— much, much smaller! You try to stand up, but you can't seem to keep your balance, *standing on your hind legs.* You try to cry out, but your brain can only think—*run, eat, hide,*—like the mouse you are.

The End

You turn to leave.

"Block the way, Lena," Mrs. Bigley shrieks.

A slim young woman dressed in a short black dress appears in front of you. Although she holds a carving knife, she stares at you with fear in her eyes.

"I can't, I can't, Mrs. Bigley," she cries. "I can't anymore—you WITCH!"

She is screaming now at Mrs. Bigley, and you turn and look at the old woman, who looks even paler and more hateful than before. For a brief moment, you see the image of a black cat in her eyes before they close as she collapses in a heap on the floor. You and Lena bend down and examine her. You lift her wrist to take her pulse, but she seems to be dead.

"You've saved me!" Lena cries. "But, we must get out of here. Follow me!"

You want to run with her, but you also remember Jane is missing!

If you run out of the house with Lena, turn to page 72.

If you go back to the front hall where you left Jane, turn to page 73.

Jervis leads you to the door, muttering and shaking his head. He unlocks and opens it. As you step inside, he shrinks back, as if afraid to enter. Although you are scared to be alone in the house yourself, you are just as glad not to have Jervis along.

You walk through the huge kitchen, kicking pieces of the broken tile floor aside, and then through the dining room, with its long oak table and high-backed chairs. You call for Jane as you walk into the elegantly furnished library, where you see before you, standing in the middle of the oriental rug, a large black cat that stares up at you with intense, green eyes. It must be Melissa.

The cat starts pacing back and forth. It runs into the front hall and then comes back to the doorway and peers up at you as if it wants you to follow.

You follow the cat through the front hall and past the main staircase. Suddenly, you see someone or something in the shadows. You are tempted to investigate, but you don't want to lose track of Melissa.

Perhaps you only *imagined* you saw someone.

*If you follow the cat,
turn to page 76.*

*If you stop to investigate what
it was you saw, turn to page 74.*

"That's all right," you say. "Thanks for your offer."

"The mistress would not mind you coming in, but she would not want you prowling around," he says. "Do you understand? So you must leave here now—or I shall make you regret you ever came!"

You hurry away. Jervis watches until you reach the road before going back into the cottage.

If you run down the road to get help and find Michael, turn to page 77.

If you run down the road only until you are out of sight of the cottage, and then sneak back and see if you can get into the house, turn to page 78.

You open the window and call as loudly as you can, "JANE!"

The only response is the squeaking of the mouse.

Then you hear a raspy voice calling, "Who are you? What do you mean breaking into my house?"

You vault into the room, open the door, and run to the hall. There you encounter a tall, elderly woman, who stands glaring at you with burning, green eyes—Mrs. Bigley! But, a moment later she seems to vanish right in front of you! Confused and upset, but determined to find Jane, you continue on into the darkened hallway. As you stop to let your eyes adjust, you hear a shaky, quivering voice calling in the darkness, again and again, "Help me. Set me free."

You stand, frozen, listening, while the voice continues, "Walk toward me. Touch my hand. Free me!"

As you walk toward the voice, you feel as if you are walking in a fog. You can only see a few feet in front of you. Suddenly there appears before you an outstretched hand, pale white—its long bony fingers extended toward you. You hesitate, but the hand lunges forward and seizes your own hand in a cold, clammy grip.

If you wrench yourself away and run for it, turn to page 82.

If you say, "There, the curse is ended," turn to page 83.

You raise the window all the way, and climb in. The mouse shivers in the corner. As you stand looking at it, you notice something moving to the left of you. It is a large black cat. Its shoulders are hunched and its head is low as it stalks the mouse. Then, angered by your intrusion, it leaps aside, arching its back and hissing at you.

The cat turns; you grab for it, and your hands come down on its tail. You hold it a moment, but it slips away and runs into an open cupboard. When you look in, you see it is actually a tiny passageway.

You run around the corner and down the hall. Ahead of you is an open bedroom door. You walk into it and are startled to see—lying on a rug—a thin, tall, elderly woman, dressed in a long black dress. Her hair is reddish-white, and her face is pale white. She is clutching at her chest with her thin bony hands. She stares at you with burning green eyes as you approach.

"I'm dying," she cries. "It's too much for my heart. Too much . . . *but you will be next. I'll see to that!*"

If you say "I'll get a doctor,"
turn to page 80.

If you ask "Where is my cousin Jane?"
turn to page 81.

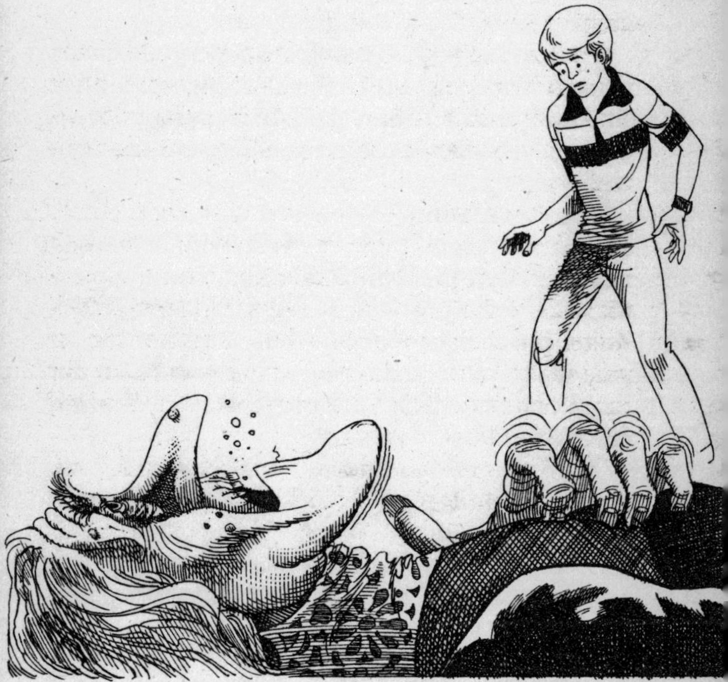

44

You call up to the cat, but it remains immobile, its eyes fixed upon you. You stare back. It returns your gaze without blinking, then arches its back, hisses, and runs off.

You follow it down a narrow corridor, but lose sight of it as it darts around a corner. Soon you come to a massive oak door. It is locked.

You try the keys on your key ring. One of them works! You pull open the door and shine your flashlight inside. There are steps leading down. Drawn by curiosity, you cautiously descend the stairs.

When you reach the bottom, you find yourself in an underground tunnel. Its floor is paved with cobblestones; the walls and ceiling are supported by wooden beams. The air is damp and cold. You follow the tunnel for about a hundred feet before it opens up into a wide space filled with casks and racks of bottles. This must be a special cave where Mr. Bigley kept his wines.

At the far end of the cave is a chest with three drawers. The top one is locked. You try another one of your keys. It works! You pull open the drawer and take out some yellowed, crumbling papers you find there. Among them is a letter, written in a shaky hand, which reads:

To Whom It May Concern

I, Horace A. Bigley, am a prisoner in my own house, held by the ghost of my wife, Melissa Bigley, who died one month ago today, and now has the power to transform people into . . .

Go on to the next page.

Before you can finish reading the note, you feel a presence. You whirl your flashlight around but it goes out. In the final, flickering light, you see a figure and, even now in the dark, you can feel its eyes fixed upon you. You reach for the rack of wine bottles and pull one out. It may be of no use against a ghost, but it is your only weapon.

If you swing the bottle at the figure, turn to page 84.

If you ask, "Who is it?" turn to page 89.

You start down the stairs toward the kitchen, keeping an eye in the direction of the cat. You reach a landing and start to walk along a passageway leading off from it.

You are wondering whether to continue on, when you hear a muffled voice calling, "Melissa, where are you? *Melissa*, where are you?"

Could this be Mrs. Bigley?

As you cautiously walk along the passageway, you hear the voice speaking again—"It's time for me to come to you, Melissa."

You round the corner and encounter a slim, tall, elderly woman dressed in black. Her face is wrinkled, but her green eyes are sharp. Her nose seems darker than the rest of her face. Her head slopes back, and her reddish-white hair is swept back in a bun. She stares at you with hatred in her eyes, and you stare back, determined not to turn your eyes away. Suddenly, she shrieks and runs down the stairs.

You follow her down the stairs and stumble through the kitchen and out into the yard. You sit down at the base of a large tree, trying to sort out your thoughts.

In a few minutes, Jane and Michael join you. They tell you they searched the house but could not find Mrs. Bigley or her cat.

The next morning, your visit with Jane and Michael is at an end. You have an hour or so before your bus leaves. You walk up the road again to Chimney Rock and stand looking at it for a long time. Then you see the burly, fat-faced caretaker approaching you, his huge dog with him, straining at the leash.

As he approaches, you get ready to run, but he

calls out, "Don't be afraid. I am your friend. You have freed me from the witch's curse!"

"What do you mean? Where is Mrs. Bigley?" you ask.

"She died, yesterday," he replies, "for the last time."

The End

You run quickly through the dining room, through the large musty library, and on to the huge living-room hall. Suddenly, you hear a noise from the dining room. You race up the main staircase and stand in the upstairs hall, listening.

Thump, thump, thump. You hear footsteps following you up the stairs. Yet when you look toward the stairs, there is no one there.

Now you are aware of the thumping of your heart. Perhaps that's what you heard; or was it something else? The ghost of Mr. 'Bigley . . . But, of course ghosts do not exist! Then you hear the thumping sound again, this time from down the hall.

Across the hall, you notice a large, cedar closet. Further down, you see a door slowly opening.

If you duck into the cedar closet and observe from there, turn to page 90.

If you walk up to the opening door, turn to page 91.

If you try to hide, Jervis will probably find you easily enough. It seems best to meet him and admit you were exploring the house without permission.

You hurry to the back door and twist the knob back and forth. Frantically, you push and pull at the door, but it will not open. Jervis has locked you in. You must find another way out.

Turn to page 50.

You walk along a passageway that leads to a large hall. The floor is covered with oriental rugs, and the walls are lined with antique oil paintings. A grandfather clock slowly ticks the minutes away, its long brass pendulum swinging back and forth.

Suddenly, a voice from upstairs shatters the silence. "Melissa, Melissa!"

You start up the stairs, determined to find out who it is. When you reach the top, everything is silent. Then you hear a cough from one of the bedrooms. The door is ajar. You look in and see a very old woman, sitting in a rocking chair, knitting.

"Come in, come in," she calls in a cheery voice.

"Are you Mrs. Bigley?" you ask.

The woman smiles and laughs. "No, No," she says. "I'm her sister, Mrs. Krim; Mrs. Bigley is my cat."

If you leave, turn to page 99.

If you stay and ask more questions, turn to page 100.

As you search the cellar, you see a door with a hole in it, large enough for a cat to go through. You turn the knob and cautiously unbolt the door and open it. Shining your flashlight all around, you are amazed to see before you a cave filled with mummies and skeletons, adorned with shining jewels. You begin to understand the full horror of the witch's curse. Can you escape before you become her next victim?

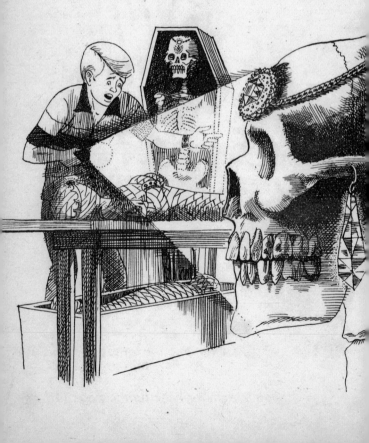

You turn back in the direction from which you came. There, standing before you, is a tall woman with long bony arms. Her hands are outstretched toward you. You are struck with horror as you observe that her fingers are long steely claws.

If you run into the tomb to escape, turn to page 117.

If you scream for help, turn to page 118.

When you call out, there is no answer. You start upstairs. Somehow you feel that the person you heard is very close. Halfway up the stairs, you begin to feel dizzy. You return downstairs and enter the study, but at once the whole room is whirling around your head. In a moment you feel yourself losing consciousness.

When you awaken sometime later, you notice that the sun has set and it is beginning to get dark.

Turn to page 71.

You start up the stairs, eager to get out of the basement. You hear the cat meowing below as you climb the rickety staircase, which begins to sway violently. Suddenly you feel yourself falling. You hold on desperately while the whole thing crashes to the floor.

Shaken and bruised, you lie quietly a moment to catch your breath. Your vision is blurred, but, as your surroundings come into focus, you find yourself staring up into the gaping jaws of the cat. Somehow you have become its tiny prey.

The End

"Do you have any idea where the cat is?" you ask.

"The cat lives in the north wing of the house," he replies. "Go to the kitchen and follow the passageway to your right; follow it all the way and you will come to a room. That's where it's likely to be."

You follow Jervis' instructions, but, as you are walking down the passageway, you step on a board that gives way. You reach out for support, but you feel yourself falling. A second later, you land with a thud on a hard, bumpy surface. Cut and bruised, you find that you are covered with soot. You have fallen into a coal bin! In the distance, you hear Jervis laughing.

Turn to page 105.

You duck and try to get past Jervis, but he pushes you back inside and slams the door shut in your face. You hear a click as he locks you in.

"Don't try to get out through a window," he calls. "I'll let the dogs loose on you!"

"You'll get in plenty of trouble for this!" you cry.

"I'm doin' it for your own good!" he shouts back.

You wonder what to do next. It looks as if you better wait a while before trying to get out. In the meantime, you might as well explore further by going up the back stairs.

Turn to page 8.

"I'll help," you say. "Do you know where we can find the cat?"

"It's upstairs. Follow me," she says. "But stay close behind. When we meet the cat, grab it. You have the power."

You follow Lena upstairs and through the upper hall to a room in the back of the house. The room contains a sewing machine, a loom and a table. There is also an armchair with a flower-print slip cover. On it, sound asleep, is a large black cat.

You pick up the cat and walk swiftly down the steps through the interior rooms and out the kitchen door. The cat tries to scratch you and jump out of your arms, but you hold it tightly. Lena throws open the door, and you step outside into the bright sunlight. The cat begins to purr.

Lena dances in the air. "The spell is broken!" she cries. "You've saved me!"

Michael and Jane come running up. They are surprised to see you with Lena and the cat. No one notices the heavyset man walking toward you until he is almost upon you. It is Jervis, the caretaker. Everyone looks at him anxiously, but he smiles broadly.

"I always knew that someone would lift the curse, and you have done it," he says. "I thank you from the bottom of my heart."

"Ended the curse? How? Where is Mrs. Bigley?" you ask Jervis.

"Don't you understand?" he replies. "You're holding her in your arms. She has turned herself into a cat—this time for good!"

The End

"Look," you say, "you need not be afraid of Mrs. Bigley. You are a prisoner of your own fears. If you can summon the will to get out of here, you can free yourself."

But Lena holds her hands over her face and sobs. When you try to comfort her, she leaps to her feet and runs toward the front door. You follow closely behind.

Then, as you watch in horror, she seems to freeze for a moment. Her face turns deathly white, and she collapses on the floor. You rush to help her, but it is too late. She is dead.

Still dizzy, you open the front door. The bright sunshine and cool fresh breeze quickly revive you. You are sad for Lena, but thankful that you have escaped the curse of Chimney Rock.

The End

You bend over and pick up the pieces as fast as you can, putting them on the dining-room table. When you bend down again for the rest of the pieces there seem to be as many as there were before. Wondering what's going on, you pause and glance around the room. Standing only a few feet away, watching you intently, is the tall sharp figure you recognize from the picture hanging in the hall—Mrs. Bigley!

"I'm sorry I broke your cat," you exclaim. "I'll pay for it."

"Yes, you'll pay for it," Mrs. Bigley replies softly.

You resume picking up bits of the broken china cat, but each time you bend over you see as many as there were before. No matter how fast you work, you are unable to pick them all up. Gradually, you realize that you are under the witch's spell, and that you must keep trying . . . and trying . . .

There Is No End

You must leave Chimney Rock. You run to the kitchen but find the door locked. Through the kitchen window, you see the menacing face of Jervis, the caretaker. At the same moment, Lena appears, holding up pieces of the broken china cat so that Jervis can see them. His face turns red with anger. You know that you are in trouble.

If you try to hide upstairs, turn to page 48.

If you try to escape unnoticed out one of the front windows, turn to page 92.

You enter the room and walk toward Melissa. She continues to stare at you intently, as if she could read your mind. She is clearly not an ordinary cat; she seems like a creature in a dream.

As you get closer to her, she opens her mouth, as if to laugh. Suddenly, she leaps off the piano and patters toward the door you just entered. She stops and stares intently at you again, as if daring you to pick her up.

*If you pick Melissa up,
turn to page 110.*

*If you follow her out of the room,
turn to page 85.*

You walk back toward the stairs and turn down another hall leading to some bedrooms, the furthest of which may connect to the music room. At the end of the hall is a large mirror in an ornate gold frame. As you approach it, you see your own reflection and, behind it, the silhouette of a tall, elderly woman dressed in black. Even in the dim light, you can see her burning, green eyes fixed on you. They seem to pin you to your place with a power so strong that you cannot move. You stand helplessly as she walks toward you. You know you must force yourself to act.

If you break the silence by talking to her, turn to page 86.

If you try to run past her and get down the stairs, turn to page 88.

The policeman pauses in the entryway near the back door and glances around. He opens a cupboard door as if to inspect it. He stands transfixed, staring into the cupboard. For a moment he opens his mouth, as if to scream, but no sound emerges. Then he staggers backward, turns and runs from the house.

If you continue to look for Jane, turn to page 93.

If you look into the cupboard, turn to page 94.

You break away and run upstairs, determined to find Jane.

"Come on," you call to Michael. "We must find Jane!" The two of you dash around the house, up and down the stairs, calling her name.

There are two places you haven't searched —the attic and the tower.

If you go upstairs to the attic, turn to page 96.

If you take the circular stairs to the tower, turn to page 95.

As you start toward the dining room, you hear a loud pounding on the back door. You run to the kitchen in time to see a burly, red-faced policeman come charging in. Michael is right behind him.

"I'm glad you're here," you cry out. "We need help. Jane is missing!"

The policeman seems to be looking beyond you. You turn and see Mrs. Bigley glaring at you.

"How lovely to have so many guests," she says in a phony, sweet voice.

"Yes, but where is Jane?" you ask. "I've looked everywhere upstairs and I can't find her."

"She must have gone outside for some fresh air," Mrs. Bigley says sweetly.

You do not trust Mrs. Bigley, and you ask the policeman to search upstairs. He obliges you, scurrying everywhere, calling for Jane in a bellowing voice, but without success. By the time he rejoins you, he is angry.

"I'm sure Jane left, and I'm leaving too," he says, as he hurries for the door. Is he leaving in a rush because *he* is afraid of the curse?

*If you decide to follow the policeman outside,
turn to page 64.*

*If you run upstairs to try again to find Jane,
turn to page 65.*

Somehow you feel the policeman will be no match for Mrs. Bigley. You head upstairs, determined to look in every room and closet in the house, if necessary, to find Jane.

At the top of the stairs, you hear a tinkly musical sound coming from a room down the hall. You walk very quietly to the door, which is slightly ajar, in time to see a large black cat jump down from the keys of a piano. So this is Melissa! The cat runs toward you. As it comes out the door you pick it up and hold it tightly.

"I know you can help me find Jane," you say impulsively.

You don't quite know why you say these words, but somehow you feel that the cat understands. You take off your belt and make a leash out of it. The cat squirms. It looks up at you with hatred in its eyes. Holding the end of your belt tightly, you drop the cat on the floor.

"Take me to Jane," you say.

The cat starts rapidly down the hall and then turns into a long corridor leading to another wing of the house as if it knows exactly where it is going.

Finally, it stops in front of a closed door. You turn the handle of the door. It is unlocked. You slowly open the door and look into a small bedroom. It obviously has not been used for a long time. The shade has fallen from the window, and paint is peeling off the walls. The room is empty except for an old-fashioned brass bed frame. Cringing in a corner, shivering, with no place to run or hide, is a mouse, which looks up at you helplessly.

The cat shows no interest in the mouse; instead, it stares at you—its green eyes burning. You feel as though you must get away from the cat, and you drop the leash and run from the room, slamming the door behind you. You run down the stairs, where you find Lena, trembling with fear.

"Where are Michael and the policeman?" you ask.

"I . . . I don't know," she replies softly. "They disappeared. I can't say where, or it will be the end of me."

She collapses into a chair and begins to cry uncontrollably. You want to comfort her, but you are angry that you let the cat go. Then, suddenly, you see it again, moving slowly toward you.

Turn to page 102.

As you approach the door to the music room, the sounds change. You hear a jumble of notes, as if a small child were banging on the keyboard.

You pause a moment. The door is slightly ajar. Instead of knocking, you look through the crack with one eye.

In the middle of the room is a grand piano, made of ebony and inlaid with gold. A large, black cat is walking back and forth on the keys. It must be Melissa.

Sensing your presence, the cat stops and stares intently at the crack in the door. You cannot be sure whether or not it knows you are watching it.

There is no sign of anyone in the room. Whoever was playing the piano must have left.

*If you enter the room
and approach the cat,
turn to page 62.*

*If you go back toward the stairs,
turn to page 63.*

You close your eyes and open them again. You cannot tell if you are awake or asleep. You are sitting on an enormous oriental rug. Before you are cliffs of wood, lined with enormous books. Tables and chairs tower above your head. Are you dreaming? Perhaps you are, for you feel very, very small.

In the distance, you see a great black cat walking toward you, one slow step at a time.

If you try to escape by running out of the room, turn to page 97.

If you try to wake up from the nightmare by running right at the monster cat, turn to page 98.

You and Lena run through the dining room, then through the kitchen, eager to get out, but as you reach the back door, your way is blocked by a burly, red-faced policeman. Michael is standing behind him.

"The curse is ended!" Lena cries.

"Help me rescue Jane!" you call to Michael.

"Jane is safe and on her way here," Michael says. "We found her upstairs!"

You tell everyone about Mrs. Bigley, and the policeman goes to find her. In a few minutes, he returns.

"I found her, all right," he says. "But she's no longer alive—a heart attack, I would say. The poor old woman has fallen victim to the curse of Chimney Rock."

"No, officer, you don't understand," Lena says. "Mrs. Bigley was a witch. Only her death could *end* the curse!"

The End

"Just a minute," you say to Lena. You run back to the front hall. Jane is there.

"I'm free!" she cries, and she runs up and hugs you.

In a moment Lena joins you.

"I know where Mrs. Bigley keeps the key to the front door," she says.

She opens a cabinet, gets the key, unlocks the big oak door and flings it open. The three of you go running out onto the front lawn, not noticing that you are being followed by a black cat, which, if you turned to look at it, would seem to be twenty times your size. Fortunately, you don't look back.

The End

You turn back and walk toward the dark part of the hall near the stairs. A thin young woman in a short black dress beckons you over.

"You must help me," she whispers. "I'm Mrs. Bigley's maid, Lena. I can talk to you now because Mrs. Bigley is not watching. I am under a curse. You can save me, but only if . . ." Suddenly, she shrieks.

You look around and see an old woman with a cane standing nearby. She is slim, like Lena, though much older and much taller. She is slightly stooped, and her head swings around like the head of a snake. Her sharp, green eyes fix on you and then on Lena, who seems to shrivel under the force of her mistress' gaze. So this is Mrs. Bigley!

"Look into my eyes," the old woman says to you.

If you speak sharply to Mrs. Bigley, turn to page 81.

If you run, turn to page 92.

You follow the cat across a large living room and hall, then up a circular staircase to the high-peaked gable on the west side of the house.

There is a door near the top of the stairs. The cat runs through it, and you follow. By the light coming through a high, triangular window under the peak of the gable, you can see a human figure huddled in the corner. It is Jane! As you run toward her, the door shuts behind you, and you hear a latch click. You try to pull it open, but it is locked!

You look around for the cat. It is gone. You bend over Jane, who is crying.

Is the cat trained to do this trick? You are certain that you and Jane are both in danger. You cry out, but there is no answer.

Hours go by. Every few minutes the two of you yell for help and pound on the door. When darkness falls, you are both still sitting helplessly, wondering if you will ever be rescued.

Finally, you sleep. When you awaken, the room seems enormous. It is entirely empty, except, a few yards away, sleeping quietly, is a mouse, the same size as you.

The End

You run back to your cousins' house. Finding no one at home, you pick up the phone and call the police.

The officer on duty tells you that Michael came to the police station on his bike and asked for help—and that one of the men on patrol picked him up and went out to Chimney Rock.

"They left only a few minutes ago," he calls after you as you run out the door.

You borrow Jane's bike and ride back to Chimney Rock as fast as you can. There is a police car parked in the driveway. You go running up to the back door, expecting it to be open. Instead, you find it locked. You soon discover that all the other doors are locked, too. You pound on the doors and yell through the windows, but there is no sign of life.

You are about to go to the nearest house and call the police station again when suddenly Michael and Jane come running up!

"Where is the policeman?" Michael asks.

"That's what I was going to ask you!" you reply.

You soon find that, although Jane and Michael escaped through a broken window, the policeman has disappeared—another victim of the witch's curse of Chimney Rock.

The End

Making sure you keep out of sight of the caretaker's cottage, you run back to the house and look in the windows, hoping to see someone inside.

As you are standing there, you hear a dog growling nearby. You turn and see Jervis' mastiff standing a few feet away, staring at you. It steps forward slowly, growling and showing its teeth. Now it is close enough to spring.

At that moment, a police car roars up the drive. Michael and a policeman jump out. The dog backs off and starts barking at the policeman, who takes out his gun and fires a shot in the air. Jervis, the caretaker, comes running up. When he spots the policeman, he calls off his dog.

Suddenly, you hear a crash. Jane has broken a window in the living room. She jumps out into a juniper bush.

The policeman walks up and stands looking at her for a long time.

"If this were an ordinary house," he says, "I'd arrest you for breaking and entering. But this is Chimney Rock. I'm glad you got out alive."

The End

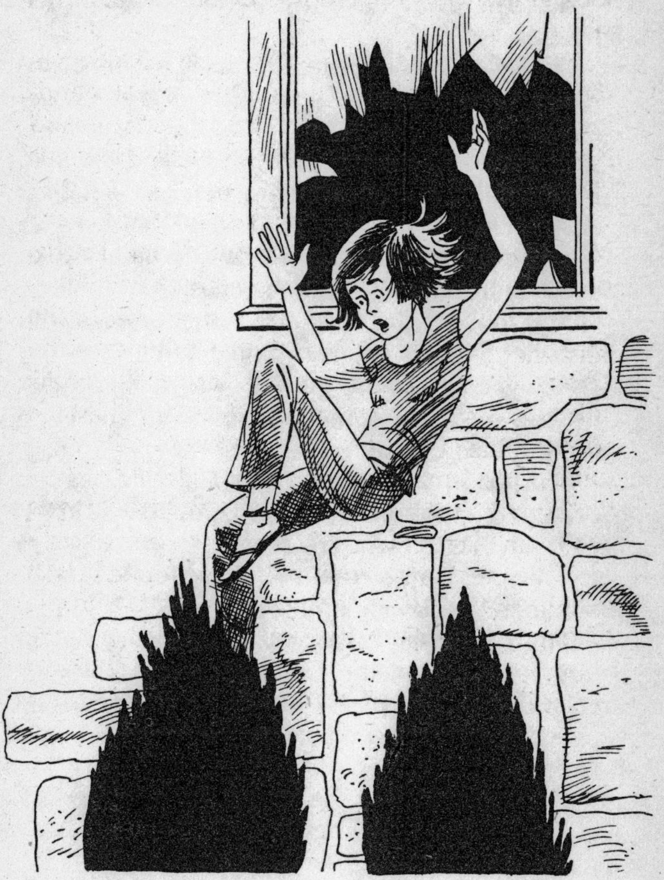

You leave the room and race down the stairs. You find Michael in the study standing next to a policeman. They have just started to search the house.

"I'm glad you're here," you say. "Come upstairs. It must be Mrs. Bigley. She says she is dying!"

The three of you run up the stairs, and you lead them to the bedroom where you just left Mrs. Bigley.

The policeman goes in first. "What kind of monkey business is this?" he cries.

You look on the floor and rub your eyes with disbelief. Mrs. Bigley is nowhere to be seen. Instead, lying on the rug—exactly where Mrs. Bigley was—is a cat, the same one you were chasing a few minutes before.

The policeman becomes angry. He accuses you of playing a joke on him. He tells you to wait in the hall with Michael while he searches the upstairs. A few minutes later he returns, having found no sign of either Mrs. Bigley or Jane.

The policeman takes you back to the station house, where you are charged with malicious mischief. These charges are eventually dropped. The police, however, have a much bigger case on their hands. Jane has completely disappeared.

The End

"You have no power over me," you cry. "Look me in the eye and tell me—*where is my cousin Jane?*"

"You've ruined everything!" Mrs. Bigley cries.

"Bring Jane back!" you insist.

"Very well," Mrs. Bigley says, her voice brittle with anger. "I can't have her. I have no life left—no life of any kind. *You* can have her!"

Her green eyes shut tightly. Her face reddens and then turns very pale.

Suddenly, you hear a girl's voice crying, "Help—where am I?"

You run into the hall and almost crash into Jane. She is overjoyed to find you. The two of you rush downstairs where you meet Michael and a policeman.

When he hears your story, the policeman runs upstairs. He returns a few moments later, his face taut, his voice shaking as he speaks. "Mrs. Bigley is dead. You three should never have come into this house. You probably frightened her so much that it brought on a heart attack. I should have you booked on half a dozen counts, but I think you've all learned your lesson."

Jane says she feels ill, and the policeman drives her home. She recovers in a few days, but she is unable to remember what happened to her in Chimney Rock.

Next time you come to visit your cousins, you find the house has been torn down. The new owners plan to build an apartment building on the property, and Jervis has moved away.

"Funny thing," Michael tells you, "they never found Mrs. Bigley's cat."

The End

You tear down the stairs, but in your haste you trip and fall, smashing your head on a post at the foot of the banister. You sit dazed for a moment, rubbing the growing lump on your forehead.

Pulling yourself together, you make your way outdoors into the welcome sunshine. By the time you return to your own home, your bump has disappeared, but in its place is a reddish mark about the size of a half dollar, the mark of the witch's curse!

The End

The ghost is gone, dissolved it seems, by the bright rays of sunlight suddenly streaming through the windows. Was it your words that dispelled the apparition, or the sun bursting from behind a cloud? In any event, you leave Chimney Rock with a light heart, thinking that the best way to escape a curse is to free someone else from it—even a ghost.

The End

You lunge forward and swing the wine bottle, striking something. The bottle breaks, and wine splatters all over you. A voice cries out—it's Michael. He screams.

"It's me!" you cry. "I'm sorry. I thought you were going to get me."

You shine your light on Michael's head. Fortunately, he seems not to be injured.

"Follow me closely," you say. "We'll get out of here."

Suddenly, you hear a roaring sound. Clouds of dust rise around you. Loose dirt scatters down around you. You shine your light toward the tunnel; it is blocked off, but there is light coming through from above. Suddenly, the roof of the tunnel is caving in. You are being buried alive!

"Don't worry," a voice calls down. "I'm a policeman! I've radioed for help. We'll have you out of there soon."

But even as you hear his words, you are gasping your last breath, another victim of the curse of Chimney Rock.

The End

You follow Melissa down the hall, around the corner and along a narrow passageway. The dirty, white plaster walls are chipped, and the floor is strewn with bits of plaster and other debris. At the end of the hall is a staircase leading up to an attic. Melissa starts up it and you follow. When you get to the top, she runs between your legs and darts down the stairs again. Before you can even turn around, the door slams shut in front of you. You are locked in.

Turn to page 107.

You whirl around and face her.

"Mrs. Bigley," you say loudly.

"How nice it is to have visitors," she replies in a raspy voice. "You've been in the house quite a while haven't you? But you've been running around as quietly as a mouse. I hardly knew where to find you. Well, now that you're here, come with me to the pantry. I have some very good cheese and crackers I know you will like."

Turn to page 37.

You turn and try to run past Mrs. Bigley. But you feel yourself falling. You look toward her as you try to regain your balance. You can't take your eyes off her. Your head hits the woodwork, not hard, but hard enough to make you dizzy. You can hardly keep your balance again, but you start to run down the stairs toward the front door.

Turn to page 48.

"It's me—Michael," the voice replies.

You are both relieved that the other is not a ghost. Your flashlight flickers on and off.

"My flashlight is getting weaker, and it wasn't very bright to begin with," you say. "Let's get out of here!"

You shake your flashlight and it flickers on. As you lead the way through the passageway, you hear a roaring sound. The tunnel is caving in behind you. You and Michael are soon covered with dust. Coughing and gasping, you make it back into the house and, finally, out into the fresh air.

Once outside, you almost stumble on Jane, who is lying near the door, clutching her ankle, grimacing with pain.

"I fell trying to climb down the vine," she says. "I twisted my ankle."

Only then you notice a policeman has arrived.

"What a sorry sight the three of you are," he says. "You don't know it, but you were lucky to get out alive. Now get out here, and never come back to Chimney Rock!"

The End

You step into the cedar closet and swing the door half-shut so that you can watch through the crack between the hinges. The other door slowly opens, as if someone has come out. You see no one, but you feel a strong draft of air. The door to your closet slams shut. You try to open it, but you are locked in. You yell for help, but beyond the double-thick walls of the cedar closet, your voice sounds like nothing more than the moaning of the wind.

It is a big closet—with enough air to last you two or three hours.

The End

You walk to the slowly opening door. As it opens wide, you feel a blast of air. You look inside. The window is broken. A strong breeze is blowing in.

When you realize it was only the wind that opened the door, you laugh out loud, but stop abruptly as you hear a cry from the hall. You step through the doorway. There before you, lying on the floor, clutching at his chest, is a policeman!

"My heart," he cries.

A moment later, he is dead. A few feet away at the top of the stairs, Michael is standing, open-mouthed.

"It was *you*," he says. "I thought it was a ghost! And I guess the policeman did too."

The End

You dart past Lena and run to the part of the dining room facing the front of the house. You unlatch a window and try to raise it, but it is hopelessly jammed. You try another. You shake the next window as hard as you can but your hand slips and goes through the glass. Your hand is slashed. Now you are desperate. You pick up a small, ladderback chair and use it to pound at the window, determined to knock out the wooden crosspieces so you can escape. Your movements increase your bleeding, and you begin to feel faint.

You call for help through the broken window. With a final effort, you knock out the crosspieces, scramble up onto the windowsill and leap out into the juniper bushes below.

Michael and Jane come running up. Michael rips off his shirt and bandages your arm. They help you back to their house and call an ambulance to take you to the hospital.

Later, standing at your bedside, your doctor says—"You will always have a scar by which to remember the curse of Chimney Rock."

The End

As you pass through the library in your search for Jane, you are surprised to feel a cold draft of air coming from the great stone fireplace. With its opening framed by huge rough stones, it looks like the entrance to a cavern. You walk up close and stare into the cold, black depths of the great chimney. You are about to turn away when you are startled by a long low moaning sound. Is it just the wind or is it a human cry? Could it be Jane, somehow trapped inside? You crouch and crane your neck to see. The air feels cold and damp. You shiver a moment, and at that moment a hand clutches your shoulder from behind. You whirl around to face your attacker; but it is Jane!

"I couldn't find you," she says. "Why, you are shivering! It's so cold here. Let's get out."

In a few moments you and Jane are safely outside in the warm sunlight. Michael is waiting to greet you. Your visit with them lasts longer than you expected, because you have to spend the next week in bed with pneumonia.

"If it weren't for antibiotics," your doctor tells you, "you would be remembered in this town as another victim of the curse of Chimney Rock."

The End

You walk up to the cupboard and fling open the door. On the shelf in front of your eyes is a stuffed mouse, surrounded by twigs and leaves as if in its natural setting. The mouse is standing with one tiny paw resting on a piece of bark. Your mouth falls open in disbelief when you read the brass plaque next to the mouse on which is inscribed *Horace I. Bigley (1921—1979)*.

Bewildered and confused, you stagger out of Chimney Rock. A few minutes later, two more policemen arrive. They search the house, but they are unable to find Jane. You have a sinking feeling you may never see her again.

The End

HORACE I. BIGLEY
1921 - 1979

You climb the main staircase. After exploring the hallways, you find the spiral stairs leading up to the tower. You run up, whirling around and around the center pole so fast that you are almost dizzy by the time you reach the top of the tower—a small, square room with large windows on each side. You have a fine view of the grounds, the road and the surrounding countryside.

There is no sign of Jane, but you watch with interest as a police car pulls up next to the one already there. A moment later, you see Jane, Michael, and the first policeman running. Even from the tower, you can see they are very agitated. Jane stumbles, and the policeman helps her into the car. Michael stands, looking up at the house, a blank look on his face. Then the second policeman guides Michael into the car, and they drive away.

You are glad your friends are safe, but you are frightened. You want to leave Chimney Rock as quickly as possible. As you start climbing down the spiral staircase, you hear the meowing of a cat, at first distant, then closer, coming up the stairs.

If you decide to go down the stairs, turn to page 106.

If you decide to climb out the window, jump to the roof, and then find your way down from there, turn to page 108.

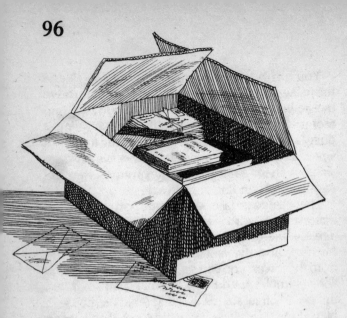

You hurriedly climb the two flights of stairs to the attic. It is empty except for a large cardboard box containing a few old books and letters. One book strikes your eye. It is titled *The Curse of Chimney Rock*.

You open it and start to read. The book starts by explaining that the first owner, Elizabeth Bigley, was struck by lightning. Her son, Charles Bigley, was killed when he fell off the roof. His daughter, Melissa, "mysteriously disappeared."

You look up from the book for a moment, wondering what happens to people who "mysteriously disappear." Suddenly you sense that the whole attic and everything in it is growing much larger, but in an instant you realize that it is you who are shrinking. You are dimly aware that no one will ever see you again.

The End

You run out of the room and into a hall. Everything seems its right size again! You have awakened from the dream, though you don't remember waking up. You must find out what's going on in this strange house.

Turn to page 10.

You run toward the cat. It looks as big as a tiger.
As it springs, you realize that this is not a dream
at all. For you, it is . . .

The End

You wonder whether or not this is Mrs. Bigley. If it is, she must be crazy. You step out in the hall and are surprised to hear the sound of someone playing a piano in a room down the hall. You go to investigate.

Turn to page 69.

"But I thought Mrs. Bigley was a person, not a cat," you exclaim.

"Indeed she is a person," Mrs. Krim says cheerfully, "when she is not a cat."

"You don't mean that she can change into a cat?" you ask.

"Let's just say that Mrs. Bigley leads a double life. You see—she is a witch," Mrs. Krim replies.

"A witch!" you exclaim.

She beckons you closer.

"You are young," she says, "and I am old. You must understand that there are things that people don't talk about, so you never learn about them except through experience—sometimes horrible experience."

"What do you mean?" you ask.

Mrs. Krim fixes her steely, gray eyes on you and waits for you to meet her gaze before continuing.

"When my sister was a little girl, she wanted to be a cat. She had a cat of her own, and she named the cat Melissa—after herself! After the cat died, my sister missed her so much that she would often pretend that *she* was the cat. Gradually, my sister's personality changed. She began to act more and more like a cat—and even to look like a cat. Then, one day . . ."

Go on to the next page.

Suddenly, Mrs. Krim looks up, her face taut with fear.

"Run to the window and jump!" she cries. "Jump for your life!"

You have no time to think. You throw open the window and jump, landing on the ground with a terrible thud. A shooting, stabbing pain flashes through your left arm. Michael and a policeman come running up.

"You have a broken arm," the policeman tells you a moment later. "That marks you as another victim of the curse of Chimney Rock."

The End

You are swept by fear. You feel as if there are bars around you preventing your escape. The cat moves closer. It jumps up on a table and glares at you.

If you close your eyes to gather your wits and strength, turn to page 71.

If you shout and threaten to hit the cat, turn to page 103.

When you shout, the cat hisses at you, jumps down, and scampers out of the room. You breathe a sigh of relief.

You run out of the room and wander through a winding corridor that leads to a narrow flight of stairs. You start down them, reasoning that these are probably the back stairs to the kitchen, and this is the best route out of the house.

Turn to page 25.

You wait anxiously, trying to think of some way to get out. Every once in a while, you call for help. Finally, you hear an answering voice that sounds almost next to you and yet far away at the same time. You grope around and feel a metal surface. You realize you are holding on to the end of a coal chute.

"Help!" you yell up the chute. In a moment, a voice answers. It's Michael! You take hold of the chute and work your way in. You find you can climb it. At the top is a thin wooden door. You push it open and climb into a back entryway to the house.

"I'm glad *you're* not a ghost!" Michael says when he sees you.

"I'm glad too," you reply. "Just the same, I don't plan to return to Chimney Rock—ever!"

The End

You grit your teeth and run down the stairs. The cat looks up, hissing and glaring at you with hatred. You feel dizzy and weak in the knees, but you run past it down to the hallway, down the main staircase, and then to the kitchen door.

Just as you are about to escape outside, you feel yourself being pulled slowly back as if by some invisible hand. What power can it be that has stopped you in your tracks? You turn and look into

a pair of ghostly eyes surrounded by a round gray glow. From its mouthless form you hear this command: *"Leave at once. If ever again you look at Chimney Rock, my fate will be your fate."*

You rush out into the bright sunshine, thankful to be free and resolve never to look back at Chimney Rock!

The End

or

If you take one last look despite the warning, turn to page 119.

You yell for help, but there is no answer. Hours go by. Every few minutes you yell and pound on the door. Darkness falls, and you sit helplessly, wondering if you will ever be rescued. Finally, you fall asleep.

When you awaken, *if you are not still dreaming,* the room seems to have expanded a hundredfold. It is entirely empty, except, a few yards away, sleeping quietly, is a mouse the same size as you.

The End

You try to lift up the window. It is jammed, and you cannot budge it. The meowing comes closer. You try the next window and, with great effort, open it. It is a long jump down to the roof, but you are sure you can make it. You climb out on the sill and get ready to spring, gauging your distance carefully, thinking how you will land.

You glance back and see, perched on the railing at the top of the stairs, the black cat, its green eyes staring at you with an intensity you have never sensed before. Through its eyes, some great evil seems revealed to you.

You jump, but you land off balance. The pitch of the roof is steeper than you realized. You can't stop yourself from falling—all the way.

A few hours later, two policemen find your body. They look at each other, and shake their heads. Speaking at the same time, they say the same thing—"It's the curse of Chimney Rock."

The End

You pick Melissa up and walk swiftly downstairs and out of the house. Michael and Jane are waiting in the rear yard. When they see you, they come running. Right behind them is Jervis, the caretaker.

"I always knew someone would lift the curse," Jervis says. "You are the one who has done it and I'm the one who will get the reward."

Jervis starts to take the cat from you, but it bristles and hisses at him. When he backs away, the cat nestles down again in your arms.

"Melissa is choosing you as its new owner. She's yours to keep if you want her," he says, as he turns abruptly and starts back toward his cottage.

"Do you think there really is a reward?" Jane asks.

"If there is, why should Jervis get it?" Michael adds.

You were wondering the same thing yourself.

If you decide to go to Jervis' cottage and ask what he meant about a reward, turn to page 111.

If you decide to go back with Michael and Jane to their house and leave Melissa at Chimney Rock, turn to page 112.

If you decide to go back with Michael and Jane to their house and take Melissa along with you, turn to page 113.

"I'm going to find out what he's talking about," you say to your cousins, and you let Melissa down and walk toward the cottage. Michael and Jane follow.

For a while your knocking goes unanswered, but finally Jervis opens the door. At first he doesn't seem anxious to talk to you, but, when you persist in your questioning, he explains that he was promised a reward if he would live in the cottage and take care of the cat until it chose a new owner.

"You ended the curse. But don't think you're going to get any of the reward," he shouts, as he slams the door in your face.

The three of you search for Melissa, but she is nowhere to be seen. It's getting late, so you start home, pausing just long enough to take a last look back at Chimney Rock. But when you do, there is nothing to be seen except a meadow filled with wild flowers. The curse of Chimney Rock itself was no more than a dream!

But what is not a dream is the large black cat, walking toward you out of the meadow, then brushing up against your legs, as if to announce that you are its new owner—for better or for worse.

The End

You let Melissa down and shoo her away. She looks up at you reproachfully and scampers off into the woods. You and your cousins head back to their house.

That evening you ask your aunt and uncle whether they have heard anything about a reward for ending the curse of Chimney Rock. Your uncle laughs at the idea, but he says that if anyone knows, it would be the Bigley's family lawyer, Gilliam Prem.

If you decide to consult Gilliam Prem before ending your visit, turn to page 114.

If you decide to end your visit and have nothing further to do with Chimney Rock, turn to page 116.

Melissa seems grateful when you bring her back to your cousins' house and give her a bowl of warm milk.

Tomorrow your visit with Michael and Jane will end, and you must decide whether or not to take Melissa home with you.

If you leave Melissa with Michael and Jane, turn to page 120.

If you take her home with you, turn to page 121.

The next morning, after a long wait, you are admitted to the musty office of Gilliam Prem, Esquire.

You tell him everything that happened and, when you finish, ask whether there is a reward for ending the curse of Chimney Rock.

Mr. Prem tilts back in his black leather chair and puffs on his pipe before replying.

"Well," he finally says, "it's true I told Jervis that he would get a reward of $1,000 if he stayed in the cottage and fed the cat until it died or chose a new owner. I have been following the instructions in Mrs. Bigley's will. But there is another reward Jervis doesn't know about: Mrs. Bigley's will also provides that if the cat chooses a new owner, *who is willing to take the cat,* then that person will become the owner of the cat—and of Chimney Rock."

"By the way, you may not realize it," Mr. Prem continues, "but now that the curse is ended, Chimney Rock is worth a quarter of a million dollars!"

Suddenly, you realize that, if you had not let Melissa go, that's how much *you* would be worth!

The End

The next morning you bid your cousins good-by and thank them for entertaining you.

A few weeks later, you get a letter from Jane saying that Melissa has vanished completely, Jervis has moved away, and that Chimney Rock is to be turned into an apartment house.

You wonder whether the people who live there will feel the power of the curse of Chimney Rock.

The End

You retreat into the tomb, leaping among the brittle bones. The witch follows. She comes at you, but you dart past her, bolt the door and dash up the rickety stairs, grateful to have escaped the curse of Chimney Rock.

The End

You scream for help. As the witch raises her horrible arms, you back away, but all your strength is leaving you. Losing your balance, you fall backward, and take your grisly place among the victims of the curse of Chimney Rock.

The End

Aaa
a

a

a

a

a
h

a
c
h
t
THUNK

Next morning you thank your cousins and say good-by.

A couple of weeks later you receive from Jane a most amazing letter. She says that Mrs. Bigley's will provided that, if the cat chose a new owner who was willing to keep it, such person would become the owner of the cat—and of Chimney Rock. Because they kept Melissa, Michael and Jane now own Chimney Rock, and, because the witch's curse is ended, it's worth a quarter of a million dollars!

The End

Next morning, with a suitcase in one hand and a cat carrier in the other, you thank your cousins and bid them good-by.

A couple of weeks later you get a most amazing letter from Gilliam Prem. It says that Mrs. Bigley's will provided that, if the cat chose a new owner who was willing to keep it, that person would become the owner of the cat—and of Chimney Rock! Because you kept Melissa, you are the new owner of Chimney Rock. Because the curse is ended, it's worth about a quarter of a million dollars, and so are you!

The End